Gratefulness In Random Thoughts

VERONICA ATANANTE KUNG

ReadersMagnet, LLC

Gratefulness in Random Thoughts
Copyright © 2020 by Veronica Atanante Kung

Published in the United States of America
ISBN Paperback: 978-1-952896-54-5
ISBN eBook: 978-1-952896-55-2

All rights reserved. No part of this publication may be reproduced, stored in a retrieval system or transmitted in any way by any means, electronic, mechanical, photocopy, recording or otherwise without the prior permission of the author except as provided by USA copyright law.

The opinions expressed by the author are not necessarily those of ReadersMagnet, LLC.

ReadersMagnet, LLC
10620 Treena Street, Suite 230 | San Diego, California, 92131 USA
1.619.354.2643 | www.readersmagnet.com

Book design copyright © 2020 by ReadersMagnet, LLC. All rights reserved.
Cover design by Ericka Obando
Interior design by Shemaryl Tampus

CONTENTS

Gratefulness in Random Thoughts vii

Saturday, September 1, 2018 1

Friday, September 7, 2018 3

Monday, September 17, 2018 5

Tuesday, June 11, 2019 6

Saturday, August 10, 2019 7

Monday, August 12, 2019 8

Tuesday, August 13, 2019 9

Sunday, September 22, 2019 10

Wednesday, October 16, 2019 12

Saturday, October 26, 2019 14

Wednesday, October 30, 2019................... 16

Friday, November 8, 2019...................... 18

Sunday, November 17, 2019 21

Tuesday, November 26, 2019................... 22

Saturday, December 28, 2019 23

Gratefulness in Random Thoughts

I know I am schizoaffective. I know I have incoherent thoughts. But, I know my illness may be a blessing because there is value in my random thoughts.

Writing is my coping technique for my schizoaffective disorder. I have included ways in which I reshape my thoughts during calamity and sometimes not so seriously bad times. As a schizoaffective fellow, you may choose to pick up the lessons of some of my thoughts or none of them. If you choose the latter thought, I hope you are not giving up with having your illness because you will find yourself in square one. I am writing to give you the idea that you need to find your own technique of coping. What are you going to do to cope? This illness has no cure. I use my writing to listen to myself better, to learn about myself and to appreciate God.

Saturday, September 1, 2018
It's 8:49 pm.

I am in a state of desolation: confusion, depression, disorientation, questionings, doubtings, darkness, hopelessness. God asks me to write about this because it is important.

In this state for two days, I have asked desperately and repeatedly for my husband's and daughter's help. They asked, "How can we help you?" I answered, "Just talk to me about anything!"

The night ended with me reading the 10th week of the St Ignatius Spiritual Exercises to my husband and my daughter. Finally, I felt inspired. I felt the Holy Spirit's presence that helped me read to my husband who normally would rather be on his cell phone watching boa constrictors killing their prey and guessing who was killing whom.

This type of desolation is common - at least once a week. After reading my journal back to myself often, it is really meaningless and a waste of time I learned. However, now I am grateful for the patience and tolerance of my husband and Hannah.

Friday, September 7, 2018
It's 8:00 p.m.

Thank you, Lord, for this beautiful day.

Living without God in my mind. I feel so solid like a stone. Nothing moves in me. No temperature in me - neither coolness nor warmth that otherwise would surround the inside of me like swimming in water. There is no life. It is a horrible feeling to be without the presence of God in my mind and body. But even in this moment, my Faith tells me He puts me in this situation to form one of my experiences. In this case, it is to be living and yet dead. Yes, I eat and drink to nourish and keep my physical body functioning. And my soul is hollow as though I was a shell without its occupant.

How long can I be dead like this? Hours, days, years? While dead, thoughts and questions enter my journal as I write. God, what have I done to deserve this suffering? Why must I go through this desolation? If you say you love all people, I have been a good person, am I slipping from your embrace?

After this moment, there was a mental dialog with God that there is a reason why this experience had to take place - to feel the grace of the presence of God.

Monday, September 17, 2018
It's 5:14 am.

Thank you, Lord, for this beautiful day.

Sometimes I am glad that I am sheltered in my memory. Only in this way I can think of God in His purity in my mind. There is no history. There is no synism. There is only the baby Jesus in my mind. There is Faith. There is the beatitude - *Blessed are the clean of heart, for they will see God.* There is only the ebb and flow of God's love washing ashore on a fine sandy beach. There is the virtue of patience as a mother brings up her child of 10 years of age.

There is peace as I write this morning.

Tuesday, June 11, 2019
It's 10:38 a.m.

Thank you, Lord, for this beautiful day.

In the morning, I woke up and I looked aimlessly, then smiled sweetly and remembered how beautiful this day can be. Towards 10 a.m., I was struggling to keep this day beautiful.

I started thinking sarcastically about the actions of other people, in a bad sense. The words selfish, envy and jealousy had popped into my mind. Sin-filled thoughts had overrode virtuous thoughts. I was so sure I was right about my thoughts of others. I began to feel sad. But how can the right thoughts bring sadness if they are truly right?

Sadness does not give me a beautiful day. So, I turned my mind around and began my thought intervention process and wrote. *Stop it. Relax. Pray.*

Saturday, August 10, 2019
It's 8:22 p.m.

A very angry man yelled at me tonight, "NEXT TIME... STOP!" I had cut him off in front of his young family when going into a driveway to Kingsburg Restaurant.

Lord, I am sorry and feeling uneasy for cutting him off. I hope he feels good. He is right.

Lord, hear me and thank you for withholding my tongue from wanting to yell back in self-serving defense.

Monday, August 12, 2019
It's 8:30 p.m.

Thank you, Lord, for this beautiful day.

I am afraid and depressed that I cannot write, Lord.

Please make this day a beautiful, beautiful, beautiful day for me. That . . . I repeatedly prayed until night.

Tuesday, August 13, 2019
It's 8:01 p.m.

Thank you, Lord, for this beautiful day.

I do not want to be well, Lord. You will be gone if I am well. You will not whisper into my ear how to write any longer.

Being well, means that I will be writing with my mind and not my heart. My mind tells me I can do without you. I wrote my first book with my heart. You whispered into my heart. I felt You. Now that I am better, I don't hear or feel you.

He whispers, "Trust in Me. I am guiding you." *A story.*

Sunday, September 22, 2019
It's 12:40 p.m.

Thank you, Lord, for this beautiful day.

I am sad again . . . There is always something I find wrong in other people that makes me feel I am better than them. The truth is that if I were not schizoaffective, I'd probably not even waste time thinking about unworthy and unhealthy thoughts. It's a waste of time.

I know, Lord, one day I'll come out of those thoughts that waste a lot of time and have a brand new mindset.

It's 9:36 p.m.

In the Name of the Father and
Of the Son and
Of the Holy Spirit, Amen.

Heavenly Father, I thank you for loving me.
I thank you for sending Your Son, our Lord Jesus Christ
To the world to save and set me free.
I trust in your power and grace that sustain and restore me.

Loving Father, touch me now with your healing hands,
For I believe your will is for me to be
    well in mind, body, soul and spirit.
Cover me with the most precious blood of Your Son,
Our Lord Jesus Christ,
From the top of my head
To the soles of my feet.
Cast anything that should not be in me.
Root out any unhealthy and abnormal cells.
Open any blocked arteries or veins
And cleanse any infections
By the power of Jesus' precious blood.
Let the fire of your healing love pass
    through my entire body,
To heal and make new cells to
    replace any damaged areas,
So that my body will function properly
    the way you created it to function.
Touch also my mind and my emotion, even
    the deepest recesses of my heart.
Saturate my entire being with Your
    presence, love, joy and peace.
And draw me even closer to you,
    every moment of my life.
And Father, fill me with Your Holy Spirit
    and empower me to do your words,
So that my life will bring glory and
    honor to Your Holy Name.
I ask this in the Name of the Lord Jesus Christ. Amen.
Saint Padre Pio's prayer.

Wednesday, October 16, 2019
It's 7:08 a.m.

Thank you, Lord, for this beautiful day. It has been one week since I feel very sad throughout the day.

Today, I am better. It started off with a light in the sky; my father's wound healing well; Patrick Madrid, commenting that nowadays schools teach differently about Columbus Day; and, my husband making a healthy cup of apple cider vinegar for me.

My illness really makes an adverse difference in how I perceive my day. Thank you for this beautiful day.

It's 9:39 a.m.

If schools can change history by changing what they teach to children, I can change my whole history by writing a book and change my sad thoughts . . .

I am often lost BUT
God made the stars to guide me.
I often feel empty BUT
God created the beauty in life of a full moon.
I often feel empty BUT
God created the peaceful life around me.
I often feel lonely BUT
God gave me Hannah.
I am sometimes selfish BUT
God gave shellfish so I'd change my selfishness
(because I have a similar distaste for selfishness)
I often feel obsolete BUT
God gave me Hannah and my husband.

There is hope in Random Thoughts.
My illness maybe a blessing.

Saturday, October 26, 2019
It's 9:17 p.m.

Thank you, Lord, for this beautiful day.

What kind of a mother am I? I asked this myself many times when I had thoughts that would demolish her self confidence utterly. I prayed and prayed these thoughts would not become words out of my mouth and for God to heal my mind.

Hannah and her friends held a little dance competition tonight and one friend disqualified herself . . . another disqualified herself . . . and Hannah was the last person standing. Her friend Abigail said that Hannah should go on the American Got Talent Show.

Hannah had told me all this and I opened my mouth with no gratitude in my mind and said, "Abigail thinks you are a really good dancer." Hannah took this in and was on cloud nine.

GRATEFULNESS IN RANDOM THOUGHTS

Thank you, Lord, for putting the right words in my mouth.

Wednesday, October 30, 2019
It's 8:22 a.m.

Thank you, Lord, for this beautiful day.

Two days ago, I was stressing out about a meeting I had with the Technology Division. I was stressed enough to have involuntary muscle movements all through dinner. I hit my plate with a fork I was holding. I clenched my fists up in the air without reason.

My daughter became silent as she watched me with these movements and asked, "Were those involuntary?" Stressed, I said, "Yes . . ." She did not stop there. She began making funny faces that made me smile. I smiled because I never ever got that kind of reaction from anyone trying to make me feel better. I said, "Thank you, Hannah. You know what I need right now to make me feel better (less stressed)."

Lord, thank you for blessing me with this child.

Then, there was my husband. He is a blessing to me but that evening he didn't say anything that made me feel less stressed. In fact, my reaction was down to picking a fight with him with everything he said. Then, he sat down with a cup of tea in his hand and just kept silent while Hannah gave me therapy. I believed he was listening with the intention of not giving up on helping me feel less stress.

Finally, he told me that I should just be myself in the meeting (tomorrow) that was stressing me. I felt much relief and took my place next to him on the sofa with my cup of apple cider vinegar.

It's 4:37 p.m.

Thank you, Lord, for this beautiful day.

I definitely offended my friend today. After all she has done for me, her boss pushed me to the limit and I left my friend to take all the blame for being late to the meeting. She was late and, although I was late too, I made sure I was not blamed at all.

I felt guilty and afraid I lost a good friend then I thought, why should I care about what she thought of me because my intention of not protecting her was not intentional? My worries dissipated and I also thought despite my fear of losing a friend, I am strong and can continue without her full support in life.

· · ·

I did it - what a beautiful day you've given me Lord. You gave me the strength mentally to complete the day by not worrying so much.

· · ·

Friday, November 8, 2019
It's 9:24 a.m.

Me: Dad, I think I have a fever.

· · ·

Me: Dad, I think I look unpleasant.

· · ·

Me: Dad, I feel lazy.

· · ·

Me: Dad, I feel sleepy (in the middle of the day).

· · ·

Me: Dad, I feel stressed.

· · ·

Me: Dad, I feel lonely.

. . .

Dad: (Laughing lightheartedly) Why do you not ever say - I feel loved. I feel loved because I have you and Hannah.

ATTITUDE IS A *Little thing* THAT MAKES A BIG DIFFERENCE

It's 9:31 a.m.

Thank you, Lord, for this beautiful day.

A voice in my head during Mass.

It's Veterans' Day Mass at Hannah's school. I just didn't want to be there as I sat in the pew.

I heard a voice in my head.

Find the best time to leave . . . on the feast day of St Elizabeth of the Holy Trinity . . .
Leave after the Gospel . . .
I feel sick . . .
I can go for breakfast instead . . .

I can go to sleep until I feel better . . .
Father's Gospel ended . . .
Now is the time to leave . . . the perfect time . . . you should leave . . .

A few seconds later . . .

You missed the window of opportunity . . .
However, that's what is supposed to happen . . .

I ended up choosing to stay until the end of Mass.

Lord, whichever exit I choose seems to be okay with you. That is, either path is right.
I ask for forgiveness for wanting to leave your presence. Like the criminal crucified by your side asked for forgiveness, you said, "Truly I tell you, today you will be with me in paradise." Your love is unconditional.

Sunday, November 17, 2019
It's 3:50 p.m.

Thank you, Lord, for this beautiful day. Everyday is a blessing.

I am forcing my failures as a child into my child. I thought . . . my failures or needs should not become my daughter's life. She is her own person and has her own life. . . . But then, what is my purpose in bringing up Iana. In my mind also was this thought. *My purpose should be there to guide her the best that I can. Or, my purpose should be to trust in the Father and He will lead me.*

be the best you can be

Tuesday, November 26, 2019
It's 7:34 a.m.

Thank you, Lord, for this beautiful day.

My boss has lost her compassion to the reasons of my very honest and much needed and frequent absences from work. I had been ill with my disorder and needed time off from work. Because of pressure from above, she changed for the worse. Her boss told her that my absences is going to reflect on her performance as a supervisor. This led to her choosing between herself or her employees. She is now just a supervisor with no concern for her employees. She has been contaminated by upper management. She is unable to see my needs in order to work optimum at my job. Supervising at my work has gone backwards away from making an employee a happy and thus efficient employee.

I have become obsolete but I am happy because I have decided that my job is secondary and my health is primary. This was told to me by my boss a long time ago. I do miss her little chats with me that were filled with her compassion. (THIS IS A PARTIALLY FICTIONAL STORY.)

Saturday, December 28, 2019
It's 4:53 p.m.

Thank you, dear Lord, for this beautiful day.

Something is wrong. I am feeling sick. I cannot sleep. Sleep will make me feel better but I cannot sleep. I called my daughter from the bedroom to help and she asked me if I am able to call my sister, Teresa. The thought that popped into my head was that she must be asleep now and is with her family. Hannah asked if I am able to call daddy. The thought that popped into my head was that he was with his friends and I didn't want to alarm him at the reunion. I asked Hannah to find my rosary and she did. I tried very hard to pray but I couldn't go beyond a decade and a half. Hannah asked me to write. The thought that popped into my head was that I was far from God and could not hear him whisper. Hannah asked me to call my mother. The thought that popped into my head was that my mother does not have anything to say to me. Finally, my daughter said she would make a cup of tea for me. I often would do that for her when she did not feel well.

Then, God whispered to me to call my mother. I reached for my cell phone and called her. We talked. Then He whispered to me to call my husband. I click my husband on the messenger app. We talked.

Thank you Lord for being by my side where I would have been alone and stayed sick. Thank you for letting me know that when I am sick, it is the time I need to be around loved ones. I love you.

Coming to the end of this book, I am grateful that I am writing. I have learned that my thoughts are repetitive with a silver lining that is filled with the feeling of God's grace. It is also filled with gratefulness, increasing daily the more I write, that I learn more about myself; that I learn to listen to myself; and, that I know God is good. Every calamity I write reshapes and ends up with the reason why I continue to thank God every day. This is what I do to cope with my illness. What are you going to do? I implore you, find your own way to get out of the depression caused by your schizoaffective disorder. Take ownership!

take responsibility for your happiness

www.ingramcontent.com/pod-product-compliance
Lightning Source LLC
LaVergne TN
LVHW020453080526
838202LV00055B/5434